Gus Makes a Friend

Gus Makes a Friend

by Frank Remkiewicz

Cartwheel
·B·O·O·K·S·®

SCHOLASTIC INC.
New York   Toronto   London   Auckland
Sydney   Mexico City   New Delhi   Hong Kong

For Zacky

Copyright © 2011 by Frank Remkiewicz

All rights reserved. Published by Scholastic Inc.
SCHOLASTIC, CARTWHEEL BOOKS, and associated logos are trademarks and/or registered trademarks of Scholastic Inc.
Lexile is a registered trademark of MetaMetrics, Inc.

Library of Congress Cataloging-in-Publication Data is available.

ISBN 978-0-545-24470-1

12 11 10 9 8 7 6 5 4 3 2 1   11 12 13 14 15 16/0

Printed in the U.S.A.   40
First printing, January 2011

Gus sees snow.

Gus wants to play.

"Not now, Gus."

"Not now, Gus."

Gus needs a friend.

He will make one.

Gus makes the feet.

Gus makes the body.

Gus makes the head.

"Snow Boy needs eyes."

Gus sees Ned.

Peas make good eyes.

Ned brings arms.

Now Snow Boy is warm.

Now he can see.

"More peas!"

No more peas!

Lunch is pea soup.

"Would he like soup?"

Snow boys can't eat soup!